MW00814248

# THE PRINCE

## SKYE WARREN

# CHAPTER ONE

ONE OF MAMA'S boyfriends took us on a trip when I turned four.

We visited this restaurant that had a special mermaid show. Metal bleachers lined up in front of a giant pool with see-through sides. Mermaids swam around in time to music while I watched with rapt attention.

Even though I could see the clear little tubes they used to breathe, even though I could tell the fins were made of fabric, it was magical to me.

I think I fell in love that day.

Inside the gift shop I found a stuffed blue-green mermaid with yarn hair and sparkly scales. I begged Mama to get it for me, but she said no. We never had much money.

The next day we went tubing in the river.

The tubes were black and slippery, the water dark. Not sparkly blue water like the mermaids had. I didn't like it but I knew better than to complain, especially with Mama laughing extra loud and Mama's boyfriend drinking beers from the floating cooler. He had what Mama called a *movie star smile*, but it just made him scary.

I held on to the tube as hard as I could, until my muscles were burning. It was too big for me to lay over the top, too big around even as I floated in the center, my arms slung over the large rubber sides. The river bumped me this way and that, taking me away from Mama until I pumped my legs to get back to her.

It happened suddenly.

The water got rough.

My hands slipped from the rubber.

I kicked hard against rocks smooth with algae. It hurt but I knew I couldn't stop.

The water sucked me down.

One minute I was floating in the middle of a big black tube. The next I was completely under, black currents swirling me around in circles, like a leaf in a hurricane. I remember the fear of it, the way I felt freezing inside, even colder than the water surrounding me.

The current slammed me to the bottom, the rocks hitting my back.

Then my head.

I don't remember what happened next, but someone must have pulled me out of the water.

Mama bought me the mermaid with green-blue hair to make me feel better. I kept that mermaid for a long time. Even after Mama was gone. I like to think it means she loved me, even if she ended up loving needles more. I found her in the bathtub one night, her grown-up things spilled over the cracked tile, her eyes open, her hands cold.

I didn't ever like swimming after that, even in sparkly blue pools.

After that I went to live with Daddy in the trailer park. I think he felt bad for what happened with Mama. He had this careful voice he used with me, like he thought I might cry. Even though I never did.

Daddy brought me to his parole meeting once. I sat in a chair with itchy fabric and wooden arms, trying not to look at the other men in the waiting room. The officer wore a brown suit, not a police uniform. He asked me if I liked living with Daddy.

"It's okay."

He leaned forward, his eyebrows pressed together. He had a big nose and a shiny head, but not in a bad way. It made me trust him. Like he was a regular person. I didn't trust people who looked too slick and handsome, the kind of men

Mama dated.

The kind of men who bring needles as presents. The kind of men who disappear in the middle of the night with our rent money.

"Are you sure, Penny? You can tell me the truth."

I think he wanted me to tell him about the gambling, the nights we would go to the bar, when I would sit in the corner with a book while the men shouted and smoked and drank. The way Daddy would sometimes lose everything, even bus fare, and we would have to take the long walk back to the trailer park.

"I like it here," I tell him, because I do. There are no needles, and most of the time there's enough food. I can't trust that anything else would be better. "Daddy takes good care of me."

It was almost true when he brought me to his card games. The owner of the bar was named Big Joe, and he would usually give me a plate of French fries and a Sprite. Mostly I ate every day. That didn't last forever.

Once Daddy said I was old enough to stay home, it got worse.

He started staying out overnight, only coming back the next morning, his clothes rumpled and his eyes red. Then it was two days. Then three.

Four.

Now I watch the dirt road from the window, wondering if he'll come back tonight. I tried to make the box of mac and cheese last, but it's gone now. My tummy makes a loud sound. Daddy won't have much money, if he comes back now. He never does after the long trips. But I still keep wishing for him. Even if we were hungry, we would be together.

This is the longest he's been gone.

Worry presses down on my chest, making it hard to breathe. What happens if he doesn't come back? The same way Mama didn't come back? *No, don't think like that.* So I keep looking out the window, hoping I see his large form coming zig-zag down the lane.

When it gets to be nine o'clock, I take a bath and get into my favorite nightgown. I try to keep a regular bedtime even when Daddy's gone. It makes me feel like there's a grownup in the trailer.

I climb into bed, staring through the blinds on my window.

My bedroom faces the back of the trailer park, away from the city lights. I can see a line of dark trees that move in the wind.

Then a flicker of something. A light. A fire?

My heart pounds harder. I can feel it thump

in my chest. Darkness creeps up in my mind. What if Daddy's out there? What if he couldn't find his way home? He knows the way, but if he's been drinking a lot he might have gotten lost.

He's never been gone this long. That must be him.

*I want it to be him.*

I don't know whether the ache in my heart is hope or fear. *Both.*

Mostly I know better than to go outside after dark. Even if someone bangs on the door, the lock stays turned. Unless it's a policeman with a badge. But I'm too awake to fall asleep.

Then there's another flash of something bright through the trees.

I open the door slow, as if something in the shadows might jump at me. There's nothing, only the soft whisper of grass in the wind. No one mows around here. Weeds come up to my knees. Brambles poke the bottoms of my feet. I press through the trees, determined to find out what's on the other side.

There's a watering hole around here some-where. I've never been there. Never wanted to. But I've heard some of the kids on the bus talk about fishing there, before they moved up to middle school. I don't think they really meant fishing anyway, not with the sweet smoke floating through the brush.

The air sounds different as I reach the water. More of a gentle hum. Less rustling of leaves. I peek over a bush to see a wide black lake. It's bigger than I would have thought. The moon draws a long oval across the surface.

Then I see him.

A man sitting on the ground, his elbows resting on his legs. He's watching the water like it's got the answers he's looking for. Like there are mermaids inside.

Something stings my leg. An ant? I jump, bumping into the bush.

The sound breaks the silence.

He stands and faces me, moonlight across his face. He's younger than I thought. Maybe in high school. I think through the families who live in the trailer park, but no one has a kid his age. And I would remember him if I had seen him. There's something about the way he holds himself. Smooth and strong, so different from the hunched over way people move around here.

He's got something in his hand. It glints in the dark. Some kind of weapon.

"Who's there?" he says.

He doesn't sound afraid. *I don't want to be*

*afraid.*

But I am. I take a step back, breaking a branch.

"Come out where I can see you! I have a gun. I'll start shooting if I have to."

Shooting? Part of me wants to run the other way, to keep running until I make it back to the trailer and lock the door. But what if he does start shooting? I take a step forward.

Then another.

I'm standing in front of the trees, trembling too hard to speak. He's maybe a few yards away, but it might as well be a few inches. Too close for me to run.

"Where's your daddy?" he says, like maybe he knows him.

I lift my shoulder. "Dunno."

"You alone?"

That's a scary question for a boy to ask a girl. "Are you?"

He lowers his weapon. "No one comes here. There's nothing but bugs and dirt. And maybe wolves."

Wolves? No one told me about wolves. "For real?"

"Haven't seen one, but I have a knife. I can fight if I have to."

"You don't shoot them?"

He looks away, like he's embarrassed. "That was a lie."

I understand that. And it means he *was* scared, even if he didn't sound like it. I understand that, too. I take a step closer to him, curious now. "Why are you here then? If there's nothing but bugs and dirt?"

"Better than home. Why are you here?"

Because I'm hungry. Because I'm lonely and afraid. The lake glistens dark, looking more like ink than water. "You ever go swimming?"

"Sometimes."

He's probably not afraid of the water. "Are there sharks?"

"Sharks don't live in lakes."

Bending down I touch the surface and find it cold. "What's here then?"

"Alligators, probably."

I pull my hand back. "You fight those too?"

"Nah, they have to be pretty desperate to go after a person. Mostly they eat fish."

Alligators don't sound like fun, whether they're desperate or not. Wiping my hand on my nightgown, I move away from the water. There's a little space with no weeds coming up. Only dirt. A sleeping bag and some food. Clothes spread out like they're drying. How long has he been here?

I glance at him. "You live here."

He lifts his chin. "And you live in the trailer park."

The way he talks to me, it's like I'm his equal. A person.

Most people dismiss me as soon as they look at me. I know I'm small, maybe smaller than other girls my age. Even Mrs. Keller looks at me different, like I'm special.

This boy talks to me rough, like he knows I can take it. There are twigs on the ground. When I pick one up I realize it's a reed from the water, dried out and snapped.

I press the sharp tip to the dirt and draw one side of a heart. Then the other.

"Go home," he says.

When I'm alone it feels like I'm on the moon, far away from anyone who can help, from anyone who would want to. "Daddy didn't come back. He went drinking."

"Does he usually do that?"

All the time. "But I ran out of food."

"I don't have any food," he says.

I shrug, because that's not why I'm out here. Not now. Something worse than hunger has been hounding me since Daddy left. The fear that he won't come back. *Like Mama.*

My stomach feels so high it's almost in my throat.

"It's okay," I say, the same way I told the parole officer. The same way the boy told me he had a gun. It's a lie we tell to make ourselves feel better.

He studies me, his dark eyes narrow. "What's your name?"

"Penny. What's yours?"

"Quarter," he says, his face completely serious.

It's such a grown-up joke. I make a face. "What do you eat then?"

"Fish, sometimes. If I can catch them."

He's living on fish? Then he's probably hungrier than me. "Like the alligators?"

"Pretty much."

It would be nice to catch fish, if I knew how. If I wasn't so afraid of water. If I didn't dream about slipping under. "Did your daddy teach you how to fish?"

"No. I don't have a pole or anything."

"Then how do you catch them?"

He doesn't answer for a long time. I almost think he's done talking to me. Then he says, "How long can you hold your breath?"

The question makes me shiver.

"Dunno." I've never stayed in water long enough to find out.

"Most people can hold it for two minutes. Then carbon dioxide builds up in your blood. Your eyes get dark. And then you take in a breath full of water."

My eyes widen. *Black water. Sharp rocks.* "You're talking about drowning."

"I don't drown. Not for five minutes. Not for ten."

I suck in a breath, part surprise and part awe. He's like a wild animal. A tiger. Or maybe that black panther from the Jungle Book. Some people would think he's strange, but it's really normal people who are dangerous. With their needles and their *movie star smiles.*

He doesn't seem to realize how special he is, though. He looks almost sad about it. "Fish don't expect that, a person being so still. And when they're going by me, I stab one with my knife."

I can't even imagine getting into the water, much less putting my head under. And staying there. He really isn't afraid of anything. Not like me. "For real?"

He shrugs. "It's weird."

"I wish I could do that," I say, my throat tight around the words.

"Well, sure," he says, his voice sharp. "It's on every little girl's to-do list. Learn ballet. See the Eiffel tower. Stab a fish with a knife."

"I wouldn't have to wait for Daddy to come home for food."

He looks away. "The whole camping outdoorsy trend isn't all it's cracked up to be. There aren't any pillows, for one thing."

That sleeping bag can't be comfortable on dirt. Why does he live out here instead of in a trailer? Why would anyone choose rocks over carpet? "Your daddy never came back home, too?"

"Oh, he's still there. That's the problem."

My heart squeezes. It's bad to want your daddy to come home, worse to wish he wouldn't. Whatever happened to this boy must be truly scary. "How long have you been here?"

"Maybe six months."

Six months is a long time.

The solution seems simple. I'm afraid to be alone in the trailer without a grownup. He's *almost* a grownup. "You can stay with me," I tell him. "I've got a pillow."

"No."

It means he wants me to leave, how short and sharp he said it. Something keeps my feet stuck on the ground. The empty trailer doesn't feel safe anymore.

This wild boy could protect me, with his knife and his courage.

"Can I sleep here tonight? I won't get in the way."

He studies me for a long moment. "Get in the sleeping bag."

Only then do I remember that some men do bad things to girls. "Why?"

"To sleep," he says, his voice mean. "What would I want with a puny kid?"

That's a good answer. I climb into the sleeping bag. It's not as soft or as warm as my bed at home, but it feels so much better. Like I'm safe here, even if I don't know his name.

Like I can breathe again, even though I'm so close to the water.

"I'll see if I can catch something," he says, "but the fish aren't active at night. And it's harder to see. Pitch black. I have to go by feel."

He can do that? And it's even more surprising that he *would* do that for me. It must be freezing in there. Why would he help me? No one else does.

I want to ask him why he talks to me like I'm somebody.

I want to ask him why he cares.

Instead I say, "Thank you."

Only when he ducks his head under do I see the green corner peeking out from inside his backpack. Money. I know enough about gambling to know that Daddy will come back empty handed. That means there won't be food, not for days. Or money for the gas bill. Or the lot rent.

And I know enough about gambling to know that I don't have a choice. You have to play the cards you're dealt. I reach out and grab it, crushing the soft bill in my hand. Then I turn toward the tree line and run.

# CHAPTER TWO

THE GROUND IS soft beneath my feet, like it's made from Play-Doh instead of dirt. Rainwater pools beneath the seat of the swing, where years of feet have dug a hollow. Droplets cling to the steel bars, shaking from some unseen force.

Usually I'm on that swing, rain or shine. I kick my legs as hard as I can, until I'm flying. My hair covers my face. Tears sting my eyes. The playground becomes a blur.

When I get to the highest point, I think about letting go. Every time, back and forth. I imagine letting go of the squeaky chains that leave the smell of rust on my hands. In my head I don't crash to the ground. I keep going up and up, into the clouds.

Not today.

I was almost afraid to look at the money once I made it to my trailer, my heart pounding against my ribs. Like it could bite me if I smoothed it out.

And when I did look I gasped. A hundred dollars. Enough money to feed me for a month. Two months. Forever.

What is he doing living on the ground, fishing for food, if he has a hundred dollars? I thought it was a five-dollar bill. Maybe twenty at the most. He could have stayed at a motel in the west side for weeks with that money. Has he been gone from home longer than that?

It didn't feel right leaving that much money in the trailer, so I kept it in my pocket.

Maybe it weighs a hundred pounds too, because I don't feel like I can swing today.

Mrs. Keller has been acting strange since this morning. She keeps looking at the door, at the clock. When we go to recess she holds me back. "There's someone coming to see you."

All I can think about is the money in my pocket. He must have told someone. I'll be in trouble. My throat feels so tight I can't even speak. I stole something. *I deserve to be punished.*

"Don't worry," she says, smiling gently. "It's not bad. I told the principal how good you are in math. How you really need more than we can offer you. She got in touch with someone who can help."

So it's not about the money.

That doesn't really make me feel better.

I wander away from the swings and the slide. Away from the strange climbing gym that no one ever uses, its metal surfaces too hot or too cold. Patchy grass gives way to uneven dirt near the red brick wall. There's a place tucked into the corner, hidden from the street and from the basketball court where the teacher stands. A hiding place, but one I mostly stay away from. It's too easy to get trapped back here. Fifth grade boys are the worst. If they trapped me here, what would I do? Fight? Scream? I'm not even sure anyone would come.

I'm afraid to find out.

I hope the wild boy never trapped any girls here. Never pushed them. I don't think he would do that. He tried to help me. *And you stole his money.*

It smells bad in the hiding place, like mold and pee and something kind of sweet.

No one's in the hiding place today. That shouldn't make me nervous. Someone doesn't get beaten bloody every single day. Only most. A knot tightens in my stomach. I can't stand being out in the playground today, being around running and laughter.

A shadow appears over mine, longer and wider.

I turn around fast, but the sun blinds my eyes. There's someone standing there, way too close. How did he get here without me hearing him? I know it isn't Mrs. Keller. He doesn't have her curly hair or her dress. It's not Mr. Willis with his tennis shoes and track pants. This man's wearing dress shoes. An overcoat. And the way he stands, so tall and proud. So still. I know I would remember it if I'd seen him before, even without seeing his face. He looks strangely familiar. Like I know him from a dream.

"Hello, little girl," he says, his voice smooth like paint, spilling over my hands and turning them every color, mixing together until they're only black.

*Is he here about Daddy?*

I know my eyes are wide, hands tucked behind my back. "Hello."

"What's your name?"

The way he asks, I can tell he already knows. "Penny."

"Do you know my name?"

My stomach turns over. I shake my head, lips pressed together.

"I'm Jonathan Scott. Have you heard of me?" He doesn't wait to hear the answer. He probably knows that everyone's heard of him, even me. Almost everyone in the city owes him something. "Mrs. Keller says you like numbers."

I don't like numbers. Not any more than I like breathing or sleeping. It's something I can do without thinking. It just happens. "I guess."

"She said you can do all kinds of tricks. Do you want to show me?"

Tricks. Like I'm a dog. And I never want to show anyone.

I don't want to show him in particular.

I have the sudden flash of Lisa Blake from two trailers down. Her family had less than us, which was saying something. They got in deep with Jonathan Scott. Then one day her momma got her a bunch of makeup from the drugstore. A new dress. She looked like some kind of beauty queen that afternoon. It was summer. And that was the last day I ever saw her.

The cops came around, asking questions, but everyone knew not to say anything. She just disappeared. No one mentioned the makeup. The dress.

Even the kids understood—we didn't want to end up like Lisa Blake.

"Okay," I say, my mind racing. I can't let him think I'm special. "I'm real smart," I add, with a touch of boasting, because I'd never really say that. It's pretend.

I don't want to be noticed by him, not for my brain and not for my body.

"Are you?" He sounds like I said a joke. "What's twenty-seven times forty-three?"

I pretend to think about it. "One thousand one hundred and sixty-one."

"That's right, Penny. And what about…" Now he's the one pretending to think. "What's sixty-nine times four hundred and twenty-eight?" After a moment he adds, "Point two."

I don't want to know the answer. I try to forget, but the number 29545.8 hovers in my mind. It's like he asked me my own name. I can't forget it if I try. "Can you say it again?"

He repeats himself, slow and patient.

I bite my lip, trying to look worried. "We haven't done points yet."

"Without it, then."

I worry the hem of my dress between my fingers, wondering where Mrs. Keller is. Why doesn't she come and help me? I know the answer. She sent him here. That's how he knew I liked numbers. This is who she was waiting for all morning. I was afraid of a group of small boys, when instead I only needed to worry about one big one.

"Twenty-nine thousand," I say, before taking a breath. "Two hundred and twelve?"

My failure hangs in the air, as thick as the leftover rain. I don't want to play it dumb completely. He would wonder why Mrs. Keller called him at all. It might get her in trouble. And worse than that, he might know I'm pretending.

"Or maybe twenty-nine hundred, five hundred...and forty-five."

"Correct," he says softly, but he isn't impressed. Not now that I've gotten it wrong.

I don't want to put red lipstick on. I don't want to wear a new dress. I don't want to be interesting to a man like this. He might want me for a different purpose than Lisa, but I'm safer if he doesn't want me at all. "Do you want to try fractions?" I offer him. "We started those."

"No, little girl. We're done here."

He turns and walks away, leaving me leaning against the red brick. Only when he's gone do I take a breath, that sickly sweet air a familiar relief in my lungs. For the rest of the school day I have to keep reminding myself that I can breathe. I'm not underwater.

Even if it feels like that.

✧　✧　✧

WHEN THE SCHOOL bus screeches to a stop in the road, a cloud of dust rises into the air, turned golden by the waning sun. The Happy Hills Trailer Park is to the west of the city, nestled between Tanglewood's slums and a ridge of wilderness on the other side. It gets dark here before anywhere else, in the shadows of either side.

My backpack feels heavy with the book Mrs. Keller gave me. *Trigonometry Proofs,* it says in large block letters. The cover is wrinkled and torn, the inside pages marked up with pencil. I don't know where she got it from, but she said it's mine now.

I want to go home and look inside, but there's a hurt inside that stops me. I don't think it's only hunger. Guilt. That's what I've been feeling all day, the hundred-dollar bill I stole burning hotter in my pocket with every minute of the day.

What I should do is return the whole thing, but it's already Friday. The school gives me breakfast and lunch with my number, but that leaves me awful hungry on the weekend.

The bus lurches forward, leaving me in the middle of the road. Dust settles back around me, a thin layer sticking to the sweat on my skin.

Instead of taking the path into the park I

follow the road to the end.

Thick burglary bars cover the windows of the Tanglewood General Store. Colorful lottery posters and cigarette ads peek through the black iron. A bell rings above me when I open the door.

Mr. Romero stands up and comes around the counter, leaving his baseball game playing on the small TV on the counter.

"Penny," he says, his voice scratchy. Nothing like the smooth voice of the stranger at school.

"Hello," I say without meeting his eyes.

If Daddy comes back with money I can get candy sometimes. Kit Kats are my favorite because I can eat one and save the rest for later.

Instead I head down the pantry aisle, where the noodles and peanut butter are.

I don't know if Mr. Romero thinks I'm going to steal something, but I've only done that a few times. He follows me down the row, staying too close for comfort. I pick a few cans of soup— mushroom barley and turkey rice. When I have four cans my arms are full. I walk to the counter and set them down so I can take out the hundred-dollar bill.

The bushy eyebrows on Mr. Romero's face go up. "Where'd you get that?"

I shrug, because he doesn't really want to

know. He doesn't really care.

"Your daddy come back?"

"Not yet."

A grunt. "He's been gone a long time, this time around. What's it been? A week now?"

Two weeks. "I don't know."

Mr. Romero runs a blackened rag across his forehead. "Runs off and leaves you behind. I know times have changed, but that doesn't seem right. I don't say anything to him usually, since he's one of my best customers."

Half the trailers in Happy Hills are empty. Some of them have squatters, but they don't spend much at the store. I'm sure Daddy has bought most of the lottery tickets that get sold here. Every so often he wins a hundred dollars, but it's never more than he spent.

There's such a long pause that I think Mr. Romero isn't going to sell me the soup. Then I would have to walk a long way into town to buy something else. Or most likely go hungry again.

"If your daddy doesn't come back, you come see me. You know which trailer I'm in."

There's a lot I'll do to survive—lie and steal. But I won't ever step foot into Mr. Romero's trailer. He looks at me like he's calculating. Not numbers, though. Something else.

If I went inside I don't think I'd ever leave. "Okay."

He presses a button and the register pops open. Slowly he counts out change.

Ninety-eight fifty-two. That's what I should get back.

He puts four twenty-dollar bills on the counter. A five. Two ones. Twenty-five cents.

It's short, so I hold my ground until he adds the rest of the money. Finally I meet his eyes. His flash with dislike. I don't like letting people see what I know, but it's not worth losing money over.

Especially when the money isn't mine.

He gives me a thin plastic bag, the handles stretching under the weight of the cans. I pass my trailer and head into the woods, the same way I went the night before. I have this idea for a deal. Or maybe it's a plea. Whatever the word, I'm going to offer the cans and the money back to the boy. Then he'll have what he started with, so maybe he won't be so mad.

Maybe he'll let me take one of the cans.

When I get to the lake there's no one there. Nothing left of his backpack or the Styrofoam or his grown-up magazines. Only a few scuff marks by the water to show that anyone was ever there at all.

# CHAPTER THREE

THE FIRST TIME I cheat is by accident.

Most nights Daddy plays at The Cellar, a bar underneath an old hotel, the wooden wine racks still standing. In the back corner there's a table covered with fraying green fabric, its surface marked with burns and sticky blackness from a lifetime of games. The chairs around the table don't match—some of them stained cloth, others brown leather with stuffing poked out.

The chair I like best is cream-colored with drawings in blue—a boy chasing a puppy, a pie on a picnic table. It's like someone's happy childhood, wholesome and innocent.

On that particular night we get there early enough that the chair I want is empty. I tuck my feet underneath me and read a book, pressing my face into the pages, blocking out the voices and the smoke.

I'm deep in the world of fairies and dragons when I hear the clatter of poker chips. Out of the corner of my eye, I see Daddy tense up as he shoves most of his small stack into the center of the table.

I count up the colors. One hundred and fifty dollars in red, white, black, and blue.

My chest feels tight when I think about him losing that money. I'm so tired of being hungry. So tired of being scared.

From over his shoulder I can see his cards. A seven of hearts and a three of clubs. What could he be making with those? The other man left in the game has an ace and a jack of spades on the table. That could easily be a straight or a flush. Maybe even a straight flush.

Maybe even a royal flush.

It's wild to even bid against that. Daddy gets more reckless as the night rolls on, as the glasses of whiskey drain away. It's a sign that he's not completely drunk, that he's kept something back for the bus fare.

Even so, that's a lot of money in the pot.

He lifts the corner of his new cards. A single pair.

It's not very strong, and when the man across from us raises the bet, I can see that Daddy's ready to fold. It could buy so much food. And it's all we have left. The pot in the center? Almost a thousand dollars in clay. We could eat for weeks. Months.

If he wins.

I tug on Daddy's arm. He mumbles something, not paying attention. None of the other men pay me any attention. Maybe they think I want money for the soda machine.

My heart squeezes.

"He doesn't have it," I whisper in Daddy's ear.

Most of the spades have been played in previous games. The only ones in this hand are the nine and six. Those are in the hands that folded. A straight is more possible. There are a lot of cards that can make that happen underneath, but the odds are with us.

And anyone would use such a strong initial showing to bluff.

He pauses, his hand clenched around the last chip.

We'll be walking home if I'm wrong about this. I might be no better than him.

Daddy throws the chip into the pot.

I can see the flicker of anger in the other man's eyes. Sweet relief lets me breathe again. The cards flip over, revealing a hand with absolutely nothing—the perfect bluff.

Our pair of sevens wins the largest pot Daddy's brought home in ages.

The good thing about that night is that I could make deals with Daddy after that. *I'll only help you win if you leave money for the gas bill.* The bad thing is it only encouraged him to play deeper and harder, losing himself in the game.

We came up with signals that I would use during the game, never leaving my seat so that no one would suspect. There are higher stakes games that I'm not allowed into, being a kid. Daddy loses more money there. He enjoys them more. That always seemed strange to me.

It's almost like he likes to lose, the same way that Mama did.

*Is he going to leave the way she did?*

That was before I met the wild boy by the lake.

Before I wondered if I share the same weakness, because I'm sitting in the trailer with almost a hundred dollars that isn't mine. That boy doesn't know which trailer I'm in but it would be easy enough to ask around and find out which trailer has a little girl. Daddy isn't even here to protect me. I told him that, didn't I?

"And you're supposed to be smart," I say under my breath.

What would my life be like if I hadn't told Daddy about counting cards? Or if my brain were different, if I couldn't count them so easy?

I put the money under my pillow. It's not like I can spend it right now anyway. Leaving the trailer at night is a bad idea, especially with a strong boy who has a right to be angry with me roaming around.

If I had only stayed there I might have eaten last night.

*I could eat right now if I open a can of soup.*

Instead I pull out the heavy volume of *Trigonometry Proofs*. I feel bad for pretending to be dumb when the man asked me questions, especially after Mrs. Keller went through so much trouble. I know I'm supposed to trust grownups, but I don't trust him.

I lose myself in Pythagorean identities and inverse trig functions.

This is where things make sense. There's no such thing as hunger when I'm solving proofs, no such thing as darkness. No way to fall into the water while turning pages and twisting equations in my head.

WHEN I WAKE up the moon peeks between the

plastic slats at my window, the quiet creak of the trailer the only sound. But I know something's different. The air feels different.

*Someone is here.*

My chest feels full with relief and a stupid kind of happiness, before I realize it can't be Daddy. He would never be so quiet, especially coming from a two-week bender. He would crash into the counters, bang his head on the doorframe, and swear in loud whispers before finally falling asleep with snores that rattle the walls.

A burglar? We don't have much of anything to steal, but people get dumb when they're desperate. Maybe Mr. Romero told someone I had a hundred dollars.

Or maybe it's Mr. Romero himself, come to my trailer since I won't come to his. My heart beats wild and loud, banging against my ribs like it's trying to break out.

"Trigonometry," says a voice in the darkness.

For a half second I think it's the man from school. The one who's tall and dark, his voice too smooth and his smile too cold to be trusted. Jonathan Scott. The terror that rises up in me is bigger and sharper than when I thought it was a burglar, or even Mr. Romero in my trailer. The very worst threat. The same as drowning, my very own nightmare.

And then my sleepy mind registers something about the voice. It's not deep.

"What's a little kid doing with a trigonometry book?"

I sit up in bed. My gaze moves over the shadows in the room until I find him against the wall, his shadow thumbing through my textbook. "Don't touch that."

He flips the book open to a page, pale white from the moonlight through the blinds. "To prove an identity, you have to use logical steps to show that one side of the equation can be transformed into the other side of the equation. You know what that means, Penny?"

I'm supposed to feel bad for stealing his money, and I do, but right now I'm mad. Mad that he wasn't there and mad that he suddenly appeared. Mad that he scared me.

"Yeah, I know what it means. Probably more than you."

His laugh sounds so much like the man from school that I narrow my eyes, looking at the way he holds his head, the way his shoulders are set, the way he carries himself. Same, same, same. "You some kind of baby genius?"

"I'm not a baby."

"And I'm the dumbass who left you with my money."

My cheeks turn hot. "I'm sorry I did that. I have it here, under my pillow. The rest of it, anyway. After I paid for the soup. But you can have that too, if you want."

He laughs, the sound clanging like bells. "I don't want it back."

"You have to take it," I say, scared that he sounds so much like that stranger. "The soup is enough for me, if you leave it. And you need the money more than I do."

His shadow goes still. "What do you know about that?"

"I know you have a dad who's mean, mean enough to run away from."

"Doesn't take a baby genius to figure that out. I pretty much told you."

"Then there's the man from the school."

"What school?"

"From some fancy private school, I guess. He came to visit me at recess." Something cold touches my bones, making me shiver. There's a reason his laugh sounds the same. A reason he's run away from home. The answer comes to me the way numbers do, before I'm even sure I want to know.

Black eyes narrow. "What did he look like?"

"Like you."

This strange feeling comes over me, like it did when I first cheated. I knew I had something important I needed to do. But I didn't have a deck of cards in front of me. No trigonometry proof to solve. Numbers were easy, but people are hard. They always have been.

A boy without any place to go.

A man who promises me safety, a real future.

The proof doesn't write itself inside my mind. There are gaps between each logical jump. Unsolved variables. Unknowns. I can figure out the answer anyway. It makes too much sense.

"He talk to your class?" The boy's voice is casual, but I can hear the tension underneath.

"Not really. He came at recess. I think Mrs. Keller told him what I can do."

"And what's that?"

I shrug in the dark. "Does it matter?"

"Yeah, it matters. It matters if you told him what he wanted to hear."

That dark wave passes over me again, dragging me under. A warning. "He gave me a bad feeling. Not the same as Mr. Romero, but worse. So I told him a wrong answer."

"Good. When he comes back you tell him as

many wrong answers as you need to until he goes away."

"How do you know he'll come back?"

"Because he doesn't give up." A short laugh. "I thought that meant he would keep looking for me. Instead he went looking for a replacement."

"Did you go to his school?"

The sound he makes is hard and mean. "His school? Yeah, I guess you could say that. Learned a lot. You wouldn't like it there, trust me."

"They don't have the free lunch program?"

A longer pause this time. "It's important that you don't go along with him, understand? No matter what he says. No matter what he promises you. It's not worth it, okay? You need to believe me."

"I don't even know you."

He tosses the book aside. "I'm serious. You need to stay away from him."

"Tell me your name. And don't say it's Quarter."

"Why does that matter?"

"Because you want me to trust you. At least I should know what to call you."

"Damon Scott."

My stomach sinks. "So that means your dad is…"

"Jonathan Scott, yes. You've heard of him, then. That's good. You know what he's capable of."

Everyone in the trailer park knows about him, after Lisa Blake. The people my father plays cards with are dangerous, the ones he borrows money from even more so. But even he would never dare go near Jonathan Scott, the man who rules the west side of Tanglewood.

"Why would he want me?"

"Because he likes to fuck—sorry. He likes to mess with people. That's what he does. Moves people around on his big ugly chessboard. You know how to play chess?"

I shake my head even though he can't see me. Some of the books I've read have descriptions of chess. I know how the pieces move but I've never played. Never even seen a chess set in person. "Not really."

"Well, pawns are the front line. They're easy to find, but they can only move one way, one square at a time. A kid who's what? Six years old?"

"Seven," I say, indignant.

A soft laugh. "A seven-year-old doing trigonometry. Imagine what he could turn you into."

"What?" I asked, a little awed by the idea that I could become something. Something other than one of the tired mothers with three kids from different men or one of the women on the street corners. A girl from the west side didn't have other options.

"He'd turn you into a weapon," Damon says, his voice flat. "A bullet. He would spend years making you, and when you were done, he'd pull the trigger."

"Is that what he did to you?"

"Why?" he asks, his voice rough. "Do I seem dangerous?"

I remember the way he had looked that first night, all puffed up and strong. Like he could shoot me with the gun he claimed to have. Or slash me with his knife. Instead he had offered me food.

And he didn't hurt me now, even though I'd stolen from him.

"You're not dangerous."

After a beat he says, "Not to you, baby genius. Not to you."

# CHAPTER FOUR

FOR THE NEXT four days Damon lives in the trailer with me.

Mostly he disappears during the day. He isn't there when I get off the bus. But he always comes back at night. He works through the trigonometry book with me, teasing me when I get the answer right, encouraging me when I don't.

"Won't your dad lose his shit if he sees me in his bed?" he asks.

"I lock the deadbolt," I say. "Even Daddy would have to knock to get in. And I'd wake you up before I opened the door. How did you get in, anyway?"

"The kitchen window."

There's barely a foot and a half in that space. Only enough for the feral cats in the neighborhood to sneak in and have a drink from the leaky faucet and dash out again.

He doesn't act like Daddy. There are no rules and no drinking. But he does take care of me.

SKYE WARREN

Like a big brother, I decide. That's what it's like.
A big brother who brings food and does math
with me. I can almost forget that Daddy's still
missing.

I can almost forget that he might not come
back.

It's on the fifth day that everything goes
wrong.

Mrs. Keller calls me to her desk. "Why did
you tell Mr. Scott the wrong answer?"

I shrug. *Maybe I didn't know the right answer.*
She'd know that I'm lying. I can do a lot more
than multiply numbers together.

Her eyebrows press together. "He has re-
sources that we can only dream of at the school.
Advanced teachers and materials." She pauses,
taking a deep breath. "There would be boarding.
You would have to live somewhere else. Do you
understand?"

This is my way out. An escape from West
Tanglewood Elementary. A chance to be someone
other than the teenage mother or the girl on the
street corner.

"What about you?" I ask.

Her brown eyes widen. "What about me?"

"I could do what you did. I could be a teacher."

Her nose scrunches like it does when someone gets a wrong answer. "Penny, I don't think you realize how special you are. It's not just that you're the smartest girl at this school. You're the smartest person I've ever met, anywhere. And I wish—"

My head tilts. "You wish what?"

"I wish that you would give Mr. Scott the right answer. I convinced him to give you another chance. He's coming back tomorrow."

Curiosity sparks inside me, but it's not because of his special school. What did he do to Damon to make him run away? If he has so much money, why does Damon sleep outside?

The questions follow me home on the bus. They nip at my heels like the wild dogs that sometimes follow me around the trailer park. They keep my eyes open when I'm in bed, waiting for the soft shift of the walls that means he's come back.

I find him in the kitchen, pouring a can of soup into a bowl.

"What are you doing up?" he says without turning around.

"Couldn't sleep. Where did you go today?"

He gives me a warning look. "Around."

I sit down at the kitchen table, swinging my

legs. "Fine, don't tell me. I have a secret, too."

"Do you?" The way he asks I know he thinks it's something dumb, like maybe I'm going to tell him what Jenny Carson said during gym class again. That was only one time.

"It's about you," I tell him, triumphant.

He drops the spoon into the bowl, his eyes narrowing. "What?"

My heart squeezes a little, because when he stares at me like that he reminds me too much of Jonathan Scott. "You tell me your secret first."

"This is not a fucking game. Did someone come around asking about me?"

I'm not going to budge, even though he used the f-word. "You go first."

"Jesus," he says, running his hand through his hair. He pulls some money from his pocket, tosses it on the kitchen table. "I was getting this. You don't want to know how, because it wasn't exactly legal. And I don't like going into the city because it means there's a chance I'll be seen, but this way you won't have to go wandering if your daddy doesn't come back. You'll have enough to eat, at least."

I frown, looking at the money. There's more than two hundred dollars. How could he make that much in one day? "Was it dangerous?"

He laughs, the sound sharp and short. "Tell me your secret."

Now that it's time, I don't want to tell Damon. I'm afraid of what he'll say, what he'll think, but I can't back out now. If there's one thing I learned from going with Daddy to those poker games, it's the importance of following through on your promises.

The importance of paying your debts.

"Your daddy's coming back to the school tomorrow."

He's silent a moment, but it's not a quiet silence. It's louder and louder in the still night air, so much that when he finally speaks it sounds soft. "Say that again."

"My teacher, Mrs. Keller. She said he'll give me another chance. That I should tell him the right answers because he can help me."

"He can't help you."

"But she said—"

"I don't give a flying fuck what she told you."

"Why would she lie?"

"Because she's working for him? Because he's blackmailing her? Or maybe she thinks that no matter how bad he is it will still be better for you, but I'm telling you she's wrong."

I shrug, uncomfortable with his intensity. "I

guess."

"Don't talk to him, Penny."

"He's going to talk to me at recess. What am I supposed to do?"

"Ignore him. Scream. Kick him in the balls."

"Why is he so bad?" I demand. "Why did you leave?"

"You're too little to talk about that."

"I'm not too little!"

"You are, baby genius."

"I'm not a baby," I say, making my voice as loud and strong as I can. "And anyway, you don't have to tell me. I'll just ask Mr. Scott when I see him tomorrow."

His eyes darken. "You wouldn't."

I probably wouldn't, because it would put Damon in danger—wouldn't it? Then Mr. Scott would know where to look for him. It's such a coincidence that I would even meet them so close together. The father and the son. In two totally different places. The odds had to be huge. I've calculated hundreds of odds with just fifty-two cards, but the number of people in Tanglewood is a lot more than that. Even if you narrow that down to the west side, you're still in the tens of thousands.

And with a horrible click the calculation fell

into place.

I scramble up from the chair, backing away. "Why are you here?" I whisper.

"What?" Damon looks confused, but I already know he's a good liar.

"Is it some kind of trick? You tell me not to go so that I will?"

"I have no idea what you're talking about."

"Or maybe you're here in case I say no. Like if I don't go with Mr. Scott at school tomorrow you'll be here waiting for me when I get back."

"And do what?"

"I don't know! Whatever people like you do. All I know is that it's not a coincidence that I meet you and your father in the same week. It can't be."

Guilt flashes across his face. "Look, Penny."

"Don't say my name."

"It's not what you think."

"You lied to me."

"I left some stuff out."

"That's lying!"

"Okay, I lied. But not because I'm working with my dad. I swear to you." He stands and paces in the small kitchen, his expression severe. "And I'm serious about what I said. Stay away from him."

My lower lip trembles, and I bite down hard. It's an old trick from when one of Daddy's poker friends starts saying things I don't like. I refused to cry in front of them.

Damon's dark eyes flash. "I knew who you were because my dad keeps tabs on everyone. On people who owe him money. On people who might be useful to him. People like you."

It's warm outside and downright hot in the trailer. The poor air conditioning unit struggles against the coming summer, certain to lose that battle. But right now, standing in my bare feet on the kitchen linoleum, I feel freezing cold. I wrap my arms around myself.

My voice is small. "That's why Daddy's been gone so long, isn't it?"

"He owed a lot of money."

"You saw him?" A knot swells in my throat. "Is he alive?"

Damon shoves his hands across his chest, looking somehow older and younger at the same time. "He was desperate, okay? You have to understand that."

I blink. "Okay."

"People like that, they see their life flashing in front of their eyes. It breaks something inside them. And my father—he loves that moment. He lives for it."

"What did he do?" I whisper.

"He starts talking about his daughter, how smart she is, all the things she can do. How you help him count cards. At first my father doesn't care. He says, *not that well since you ended up here.* But your dad explains how you aren't allowed at the high stakes games. That's where he lost all his money."

My insides feel wobbly, like I'm going to cry no matter how hard my nails press into my palm. "I don't understand. If you were there, if you saw that, why did you come here?"

He shrugs, shaking his head like he doesn't know the answer. "I meant to leave the city for good. That's what I was doing. Running. Escaping. And I almost did it. I got on a grey bus heading west and pulled my cap low. Then I found myself getting off at the first stop. Hitching a ride back. And camping behind the trailer park."

"Damon," I say, pressing my hands together. This is how you pray. "What did Mr. Scott do to you?"

"What's important is that he's never gonna do it to you, understand? I'm going to stop him."

I shake my head *no*, because I don't understand. I know Damon is strong and smart, but how is he going to stop his father? And if he had any power over him, why did he leave in the first place?

"Yes," Damon says, "but you need to keep your head down. No more reading about trigonometry. No more counting cards. That's the deal we're gonna make."

"I don't want any deal." *I don't want you to leave.*

"That's the only way you see your daddy again. If I go back."

My breath catches. "But why?"

"Because he owes a debt. You didn't replace him, but someone has to."

And then I can't stop the tears. They're hot and thick on my cheeks. I hate crying in front of him, but he doesn't look like he feels sorry for me. He has this serious expression, like he's waiting. Waiting for me to take the deal.

How can I say yes when that means sending Damon back to his father?

How can I say no when it means never seeing mine?

There's two hundred dollars on the kitchen table, but it won't last forever. Not long enough for me to be a young mother or a girl on the street corner. I'd starve before that. Or I would end up with Mr. Scott.

I shake my head, because I don't want it to be true. "You can help me find him."

"And then what? We all go on the run, one big happy family?"

His tone says that's ridiculous. He's mocking me, but it *is* what I want. "Maybe. Why is that wrong? We could be happy like that."

Those black eyes soften. "It's not possible, Penny. There's nowhere we could run, not enough money or power in the world to hide us."

"What will you do?" I whisper.

In that question is my acceptance, my apology. It would always have come to this.

He knew that before I did.

"The same thing I did before," he says with a hard smile. "Survive."

# CHAPTER FIVE

THE NEXT DAY I spend most of recess in the jungle gym, in that dark, quiet place beneath the slide and behind the rusted metal wall with numbers cut out. I peer through the number eight at the door, waiting for someone to appear. No one ever does.

Mrs. Keller stares at the door, her small face hopeful. Then worried.

By the time she calls the class back inside she looks disappointed.

I don't want her to feel bad so I tug on her hand as I pass by. She bends low, and I whisper in her ear. "I don't want a new school anyway. I like you being my teacher."

She blinks like she has something in her eye.

The rest of the day I sit quiet, wondering how I'm going to play dumb. We're learning fractions right now. How do you pretend not to know something? I wish I just *didn't* know.

I wish I were normal.

When it comes time for the quiz, I take a deep breath. This is how it has to be. It's the promise I made. So even though I know that Joey only eats $1/8^{th}$ of the pizza, I write down $1/16$.

There are two questions I get wrong, which means my grade will be a B. Very average.

My whole life will be average.

When I get off the bus, from across the road, I see something dark and large slumped in front of my door. Is it Damon? Is he hurt? I run as fast as I can, kicking dirt into the air, clouding my sight.

Even before I get there I know it's not him. The figure is too large.

"Daddy," I shout over the pounding of my feet.

He doesn't move. When I get close I see why. His face is swollen and bruised, dried blood caked over the right side. The sound of his breathing fills the humid air, thick with blood and snot.

"Daddy," I say again, but this time it comes out as a sob. I can't press my nails into my palm this time. Nothing will keep me from crying now.

A low sound fills the air, almost separate from the still body in front of me. Only when I put my hand to his chest and feel the faint rise and fall, the slight rumble, am I sure the sound is coming from him.

"Penny," he says, the word slurred and broken.

"I'm here," I say, fighting to keep my voice steady. One of us has to be strong.

"No, Penny. What did he—" Daddy breaks off in a fit of coughing, the sound horrible and echoing. "I'm so sorry. What did he do to you?"

He thinks Mr. Scott did something to me. That it's the reason he's free.

"Let's go inside," I say, pulling his hand.

With a groan of pain and effort, he staggers up. Only to collapse again. I catch him with both hands, my shoulders, even my neck. A shock of weight. My bones hurt, my muscles shake. I need to get him inside. We move together in a terrible dance, falling into potholes and stumbling on the stairs. The screen door slams into my hand. His head knocks against the doorframe.

When we reach the couch it's all I can do to tip him over. He falls onto the sagging cushions with a swear word. I run to the kitchen. Underneath the sink there's a first aid kit in my old lunchbox, the one with My Little Pony on the front. I pull out cotton balls and rubbing alcohol. He probably needs a hospital. What if something is broken? But this is all we have.

I pause to look at the kitchen table. The two

hundred dollars isn't there anymore, tucked away under my bed instead. But I can still remember the way Damon looked sitting there, eating the soup I bought with his money. Is he okay? Is he beaten like Daddy is right now?

My eyes press shut, sending up a prayer that someone is there to take care of him.

Then I kneel at the couch.

Daddy looks more alert than he did before, his eyes less glassy and more focused. "I told him about you. About counting cards. He said he was going to—" His voice breaks.

I could tell him that Mr. Scott didn't touch me, but that won't help.

He could have. He would have, if it weren't for Damon.

"Rest now," I say in a quiet voice.

I learned my quiet voice from Mama. It's the one I used when she had been up too late, when men had been over, when she had a headache. When I brought her a glass of water and Tylenol.

She would call Daddy bad names for leaving her in this shithole trailer park. And then one day she put a needle in her arm and went to sleep. I had to spend three months in a group home, keeping my head down and hiding the bruises from the other kids.

Then they found Daddy. I know he isn't perfect but he's the only person I have left. Tears trail down my cheeks, but I don't know if I'm crying for myself or for Damon, who traded himself for me.

"You saw him, Penny?"

I look down. "He's tall. And his voice—it's strange. Like water."

Daddy's face falls. "Oh God. I'm so sorry."

Maybe it's mean to let him think the worst, but I need him to change. The debts and the gambling, those are his needles. And I don't want him to go to sleep, not like Mama did.

I don't want to sleep either.

And I stay awake long after Daddy snores, the pain medicine keeping him comfortable. The shadows of trees press against my window. Somewhere out there is a lake. Somewhere out there is a boy who knows how to hold his breath longer than anyone should. How did he learn that?

What is he learning now?

*I'm so sorry,* Daddy said. But I'm the one who's sorry.

Because Damon Scott traded himself for me. He's the only reason I'm safe.

And I'm the reason he's not.

# CHAPTER SIX

IT GETS EASIER to pretend as time goes by. My mind applies itself to finding an appropriate percentage to get wrong as easily as it did counting cards.

Daddy kept down a job long enough that we could move into the west side from the trailer park. The apartment was smaller than the trailer, but this way I could visit my friends after school. As it turns out, people like you when you keep your mouth shut and get average grades.

I was almost popular, but no one knew who I really was.

Damon Scott's name became a part of the city's dark culture, mostly in whispers, always linked to money or women or both. No one really seemed surprised that he had gone into the family business, that he traded in sex and violence. Even I wasn't surprised, knowing what had happened, but I did mourn him. He could have run away, if it hadn't been for me.

Then again, he's a grown man now, wealthy in his own right.

He could run away now, if he wanted to.

There must be something he likes about that life, something dark and sharp he's addicted to. We all have our own needles. We each rack up our own debts.

Sometimes Daddy would slip. Bills would pile up, only for him to dig us out again. When we got close to getting evicted I would count cards, but only once. Then twice. He was as scared of Jonathan Scott as me, so he understood the risk.

And I had my own addiction. Stolen moments in the Mathematics section of the high school library. Fractals drawn on my school notebooks, filled in with little hearts and smiley faces so that no one would suspect anything. No one ever did.

Once Mr. Halstead asked me to stay after physics, where he told me that I wasn't living up to my potential. He seemed so sincere, so kind, that I actually agreed to come to after school study sessions with him. But when he put his hand on my leg and breathed against my neck, I knew he didn't really care about my mind.

It wasn't anything special about me that they liked.

Only that I was a girl in the west side. We were only used for one thing.

And then there was Brennan. He had a crooked smile and a motorcycle, so all my friends thought he was a great catch. I could see the appeal, from an academic standpoint. His muscles were sharpened from working in his father's garage, his confidence an attractive quality. I hoped he never found out I went out with him for his books. *Automotive Wiring and Electrical Systems. Advanced Automotive Fault Diagnoses.* Not my ideal form for numbers to take, but I read them with the same secret fervor that my father bought lotto tickets, both of us desperate for a fix.

"What are you reading, babe?"

I slammed shut his book on hybrid vehicles and slipped it under my open book from Calculus class. Technically math, but it had less to teach me than *See Spot Run.* Brennan's a nice guy.

Nice enough I hope he never finds out I'm using him for his books.

"Studying," I tell him, rising up to kiss him.

He's sweaty from working. Their house is next door to the garage. "You hungry? I'll shower and then we can go somewhere."

"I have a shift at eight." I work at a sad little diner, making five bucks an hour serving barely heated food and stale coffee. It's better than most jobs a fifteen-year-old girl can get in west Tanglewood.

"Thought you had Fridays off."

"Jessica's baby has a fever."

Brennan sighs. "We barely get to go out."

Guilt rises inside me, because I kind of prefer it that way. Hanging out after school and making out on his couch. Every time we go to a party it's another chance to take things further.

Brennan wants that. Maybe even deserves it, after being so patient. But I can't give it to him. Can't end up like Jessica with a baby. I don't think Brennan would bail the way Jessica's boyfriend did, but it's too big of a risk.

I put my hand on his arm. "I'm sorry. I couldn't say no." *And I didn't want to.* "Besides, you know I need the money."

Something flashes across his eyes. Frustration. Futility? "What will you make? Twenty bucks? I could give you that if you spent the night."

My hand snatches back. "Excuse me, I'm not for sale."

"I didn't mean it like that. I mean the job's total shit and you know it."

"Well it's the only one I have." I whirl away he can't see the hopelessness on my face. There's only so much humiliation a girl can take in one evening. I stare out his window at the rows of dark windows, the broken bricks. The west side is a tumbled-down maze, not even fit for living, keeping us trapped.

There is no exit strategy. No way out.

Brennan's arms wrap around me, slick and dirty with grease but comforting all the same. "I'm a fucking idiot," he murmurs into my hair. "I know you're doing the best you can."

"I just want to…" *Escape. Fly to the moon.* "Graduate. Then we can make plans."

"Okay," he says, because he understands my desire to finish school. He has his GED and he's studying to get certified as an automotive technician. He's a high achiever among our friends. And he'll never know that my dreams are so far beyond this.

That I long for the impossible.

"I should get going. I have to change first."

He turns me in his arms, his strong hands warm with familiarity, painful with certainty. He presses a kiss to my mouth. I part my lips, and he takes the invitation, pressing his tongue inside, opening me. I let him, let him, let him. That's all I know how to do anymore.

I like his kisses the same way I like boxed mac

and cheese and my worn mattress at home. They mean I'm safe and comfortable, if not quite happy.

He pulls back like he always does. Maybe sensing I would finally snap if he pushed.

It's his own form of safe and comfortable.

His eyes search me. What does he want to find?

He traces my eyebrow, his finger agreeably callused. His expression is a little awed. "You're the prettiest girl in the west side, you know that?"

"And out of the west side?" I ask, not because I'm vain enough to think I am. Because I want to know when we resigned ourselves to this. When we noticed the iron bars around our lives and decided not to rail against them.

His smile is sad and tired. "Out of the west side you wouldn't be with me."

It's an arrow straight to the heart, because he's right. And he deserves better. Don't we both? I throw my arms around him and squeeze. We need friends in captivity.

BRENNAN TAKES ME home on his motorcycle, the roar of the engine bouncing off pavement and brick. I mold myself to his body, my eyes squeezed tight in his helmet. There's a perverse thrill as we race through the darkened streets. Both of us know this is as fast and as far as we'll ever go. One slip on slick gravel is all it would take. And the worst part is the faint sense that we're waiting for it. Wanting it. Pushing the boundaries in the hopes that we leave on our own terms, young and free.

We arrive at my apartment building, sudden stillness almost violent after the rush.

The crumbling concrete of the curb shifts under my feet.

My ears ring as I take off the helmet, placing it on Brennan's head and tapping it into place. "I dub thee Sir Brennan. Go forth into battle."

He grins from beneath the visor. "If I'm a knight, what does that make you?"

"The princess, of course."

Kissing never works well with a helmet on. Someone's forehead ends up smacked. Instead I kiss my palm and press it to his mouth, the way lords and ladies did with handkerchiefs.

A chaste kiss.

Then he's off in a cloud of exhaust, his noble steed lovingly restored and shining.

The diner is only a couple blocks away. I have plenty of time to change before my shift. Then it will be a monotony of grease and coffee, miles to go on the same black-and-white tiles with my tired feet.

I turn toward my building, mentally bracing myself for the night to come.

"Hello, princess."

The words come out of the dark alley to the side, and I jump back. Brennan insists on taking me home every night, when I could take the bus, partly because of safety. The voice is low and grave and completely new to me. If it's a stranger the best thing I can do is ignore him. Hope he goes away.

That's what they tell you to do about bullies, isn't it?

I put my head down, wrapping my arms around myself.

With my eyes downcast I can't see him, but I feel him. He steps out of the shadows, his presence like a cold burst of air in the hot night. "That's not what I call you, though. To me you'll always be a baby genius."

Shock holds me paralyzed on the sidewalk. A dangerous prospect considering it's late in the evening in the west side. Made even more dangerous because I know exactly who this is.

I know exactly what he's become.

There's a storm inside me. A whirlwind of surprise and fear, threatening to drown me. *Why are you back?* That's what I want to ask. From somewhere deep inside, another whisper. *Why did you take so long?*

"It's so much more interesting than a princess, don't you think? A pretty face has its appeal, but a sharp mind is a goddamn aphrodisiac."

When I turn to face him, he moves behind me. "I don't know what you're talking about."

He makes a *tsk* sound, keeping pace as I try to confront him. "That's not true, Penny. But I understand. You're so used to playing dumb, aren't you? It's more than a habit now. It's a veil, keeping you hidden."

"I can't believe you're talking to me right now."

"You don't have to hide with me."

"I'm not trying to hide," I say, and with him at least it's the truth. "I'm trying to look at you."

He stops moving, and I finally face him.

I must have turned one too many times, because the air leaves my chest. Nothing could have prepared me for the sight of his dark eyes—black like night. Like inky depths I could never hope to enter. Never hope to escape. He looks so much like his father it steals my breath.

Some logical part of me knows they have differences. Jonathan Scott already had silver threading his dark hair when I met him years ago. He was taller, leaner, more severe in every way. It's my heart that's somehow breaking, seeing in him the whisper of evil.

With his perfectly disarranged hair and the evening shadow on his jaw, he bears little resemblance to the wild boy I knew once. His lips have filled out. His chest has filled out too, fitting into that dress shirt and tailored vest perfectly. Only the eyes prove it's him, at once knowing and curious. Pitch black, like the night sky above the city, no stars at all to light the way.

I think I loved him once.

About as much as I despise this handsome man. He's everything my mother would have chased after. Everything I've learned not to trust.

"You're right," he says softly. "We should go up."

"You're not going anywhere with me." I glare at him, giving him my meanest look. It doesn't seem to worry him any. A smile flickers on his lips, making him look dashing.

I don't trust men who look dashing.

Amusement flashes across dark eyes, as if he knows. "Where are your manners?"

"They're reserved for people I actually like."

"Like Brennan Chase?"

I struggle to remember if I said Brennan's full name. *I dub thee Sir Brennan. Go forth into battle.* My heart squeezes, imagining Damon keeping tabs on me. "How do you know his last name?"

"It's my business to know people's names. Their likes and dislikes. Their addictions. Do you have any addictions, baby genius?"

"Do you?"

"Many. Some worse than others."

An answer that admits nothing. "What are you doing here?"

"I may not deserve a warm welcome, but I didn't expect hostility. You invited me inside once."

"That was before you were your father's puppet." I still feel guilty for that, but it doesn't change the fact that he can't be trusted. He didn't only survive his father. He became him.

"Ah."

"That's all you have to say for yourself?"

"Would you like me to deny it? Fine. That's not true, darling. I was most definitely my father's puppet before we ever met."

The seductive tone almost draws me in, even as his words confirm my worst fears. "You did what you had to do when you were a child. You're a grown man now."

"Thank you for noticing. Though I don't work with my father."

"Everyone says you do."

"They say that?"

"They say you deal in money and drugs and women."

He pauses meaningfully. "Not with my father, I don't."

It's an admission.

He does every horrible thing he's accused of doing. Every single thing I raged against in my mind. How could the sweet boy I once met be so horrible? How could someone who once risked his life for me be responsible for hurting other girls?

All the street lamps have blown out here, maybe on purpose. The only light is the moon, and when it shines over his dark eyes, the reflection makes them look silver.

He may not work with his father, but he's become him.

"And that's supposed to make it better?" I manage to ask. "That you do them for your own gain instead of working for your father?"

"Better? No, but it's definitely more lucrative

this way."

It's upsetting that he looks so clean and crisp and *beautiful* standing beside a run-down tenement. Upsetting that he looks so good when he's clearly a bad man. That his movie star smile hides a terrible broken soul. "You're not the boy I knew."

"No," he agrees. "Are you the girl I knew?"

"You'll never find out."

He tilts his head to the side, as if demurring. Too much of a gentleman to tell me I'm wrong. Except he's no gentleman. "What are you doing here?"

"I came to speak to your father."

My heart thuds. "Why?"

"He owes me money."

Oh God. *Daddy, what have you done?* "He doesn't."

I'm only delaying the inevitable, but I can't think right now. Can't deal with the fact that we have rent due in two days and barely enough money to cover it. How will we pay back hundreds of dollars?

Damon looks to the side a little. As if he's embarrassed by my horror. Or maybe bored. He straightens the cuffs of his fine white shirt, perfectly tailored to his broad chest and narrow waist. He might be waiting in the eaves for an opera to begin, so casually refined.

"How dare you?" I whisper, waiting for him to meet my eyes, daring him.

He glances back at me, one dark eyebrow raised. "Pardon?"

"You know he doesn't have a way to pay you back. How dare you loan him money? Charging insane interest rates he'll never be able to afford. How dare you?"

A small laugh. "Would you have preferred I told him no? He would have gone straight to my father, who would have charged him higher interest than I did."

"I hate you," I say, tears stinging my eyes. "I hate you both."

"And it's not quite true that he doesn't have a way to pay the money back."

The silence spins out in brutal possibility. "How?"

"He has you."

## THE END

# THANK YOU!

Thank you for reading THE PRINCE, the free prequel to the Masterpiece trilogy. I hope you loved meeting Damon Scott. Find out what he does next in THE KING!

SIGN UP FOR SKYE WARREN'S NEWSLETTER: www.skyewarren.com/newsletter

I appreciate your help in spreading the word, including telling a friend. Reviews help readers find books! Please leave a review on your favorite book site. THANK YOU!

# OTHER BOOKS
# BY SKYE WARREN

*Endgame series*
The Pawn
The Knight
The Castle

*Stripped series*
Tough Love
Love the Way You Lie
Better When It Hurts
Even Better
Pretty When You Cry
Caught for Christmas
Hold You Against Me
To the Ends of the Earth

*Chicago Underground series*
Rough
Hard
Fierce
Wild
Dirty
Secret
Sweet
Deep

*Criminals and Captives series*
Prisoner

*Standalone Dark Romance*
Wanderlust
On the Way Home
His for Christmas
Hear Me
Take the Heat

*Dark Nights series*
Keep Me Safe
Trust in Me
Don't Let Go

*The Beauty series*
Beauty Touched the Beast
Beneath the Beauty
Broken Beauty
Beauty Becomes You
Loving the Beauty: A Beauty Epilogue

Visit skyewarren.com for the complete Skye Warren book list, along with boxed sets, audiobooks, and paperback listings. Thank you for reading!

# About the Author

Skye Warren is the New York Times bestselling author of dark contemporary romance such as the Endgame trilogy. Her books have been featured in Jezebel, Buzzfeed, USA Today Happily Ever After, Glamour, and Elle Magazine. She makes her home in Texas with her loving family, sweet dogs, and evil cat.

Sign up for Skye's newsletter:
www.skyewarren.com/newsletter

Like Skye Warren on Facebook:
facebook.com/skyewarren

Join Skye Warren's Dark Room reader group:
skyewarren.com/darkroom

Follow Skye Warren on Instagram:
instagram.com/skyewarrenbooks

Visit Skye's website for her current booklist:
www.skyewarren.com

# Copyright

This is a work of fiction. Any resemblance to actual persons, living or dead, business establishments, events or locales is entirely coincidental. All rights reserved. Except for use in a review, the reproduction or use of this work in any part is forbidden without the express written permission of the author.

The Prince © 2017 by Skye Warren
Print Edition

Formatting by BB eBooks

Made in the USA
Columbia, SC
11 July 2017